Y0-DJM-475

If "A" Weren't for "Apple"
by Christopper T. Hill
Art by Landon

Book Design by Quintessential Design

Published by
Topperhill Publishing
169 Apple Lovers' Lane
Jordan, Minnesota 55352
1-800-662-7753 or 1-800-66-APPLE

Visit our website
www.topperhill.com
- Order books and posters
- Comment on our books
- Vote for your favorite picture in
If "A" Weren't for "Apple"
- See samples of upcoming books
- Sign up for our e-mailing list

ISBN 1-992136-00-5

Special Thanks to:
Mildred Sponsel, Lonnie Vander Vorste, Donna Mueller,
Joan Schultz, John Moore, Susan Kelly, Helen Meger (page 70),
The Mecredy Family, Stephen Sponsel, Jon Savoye, Dave Will.

Printed in the U.S.A

One day as I strolled
Past the voters assembling
I heard such an uproar
It left me a-trembling.

Some voters were shouting
"No A! Not for Apple!"
I saw they were angry
And ready to grapple.

"We won't vote for Apple!
There's surely no A!
All hands in the Union
Are raised to say nay!"

Now, what would YOU do
If you heard such a thing?
Would you do what I did
And start desp'rately thinking

Of US without A
And how that would be

A-2

An apple-cart upset?

I'm sure you agree.

A-4

I went to the rostrum
(the podium place)
To say what I stood for
'bout A, face to face.

I stood there and said
What I'm telling to you
'cause you were not there
(or you'd done the same, too).

If "A" Weren't For "Apple"

By Christopper T. Hill

Art by Landon

For Austin, London, and cousin Arwynn,
who are The Apples of my A's

If A weren't for Apple
We'd be in a fix.
We'd have twenty-five letters,
Not twenty-six.

You'd start off with B
In the alphabet song.
Would you feel mistaken
For starting out wrong?

First B and then C
And then D... but no A?
First "bet" without "Alpha"?
I tell you, NO WAY!

2

You'd better get ready
To throw in the towel.
It's too hard to spell
Short the Number One vowel.

Spell words without A's
And it makes you spell silly.
I tell you the language
Will go willy-nilly.

Sure, "why" remains "why"
But now "way" is "wy", too!
It mixes up me –
Does it mixes up you?

Train would be "trin"
Trying to run on a "trck".
Are you sure that would work?
Would it ever come "bck"?

"Today" would be "tody"
Which sounds like a frog.
You wouldn't be here,
You'd be out in a bog!

"Toad" would be "Tod"
Oh, that's fine (if you're Tim).
Tod better like tdpoles
And learn how to swim!

"Wheat" would be "whet"
(It's all soggy and such).
If you pour you a bowl
You won't eat very much.

"Eat" would be "et"
Like you're already done
Having your fill
When you've only had none.

Or would it be "et"
Like you've just had your fill
Of whatever you ate
When you ate only nil?

"Fare" would be "fre".
That's a bonus for flyers
And diners and riders
And trip-ticket buyers,

But "bills" wouldn't change much
They always come due
(and even sans A's
"deth" and "txes" do, too).

14

There must be a method
(I'm thinking you'll say)
To spell all our words
Without using an A.

So let's be resourceful
And trade A for "eigh".
(The sound is the seighme
As in "neighbor" and "weigh".)

"Seigh, neighbor," I heighl you,
"Eighn't this a greight deigh?"
Be heighl or this "eigh" geighme
Meigh weighst you aweigh!

Or would we do "et"
Like the French in "gourmet"
Or the name that they set
On a gret Chevrolet?

Or e-y for A,
Why, they use it in "they".
Should they have requirements
For they to obey?

Who is they
Ennywey?

Whatever they sez
Or whatever they sey,
Do we have to do it?

Well, do we?

Does they?

No reason to leighbor,
We've seen that A's better.
It gets the whole job done
Just using one letter.

I'll shout A tomorrow
And shout A today
If anyone thinks
We can throw A away.

I'll stay here through April
'til May if I must.
I feel it's important.
It's "Keep A or BUST!"

I'll shout A forever
Unless or until
We ALL have agreed
A's a need, not a frill.

I'll shout A forever.
I'll do it.
I will.

I will,
Or my name's not
Christopper T. Hill!

24

We need A as an article.
It's one: A boy. A girl.
At any rate, not two or more.
It's singular, not plural.

If letters cost money...
And all words were A-less...

Would sign-making firms

Allow buyers to pay less?

Suppose we'd start counting
At two 'stead of one.
That's crazy as A
Being locked up and done.

See, twenty-one's two
But so, too, is twelve.
At times without one's
The two's be by theirselve!

but...

They'd have to be humored,
So free, now they'd laugh,
'cause one couldn't join them
Or cut them in 1/2.

While "bet" without "Alpha"
May not seem so major,
It's not like our letters,
It's more like a wager.

It wouldn't be friendly
to B without A,
So happy together
In "band" and "ballet".

When "happy" is "hppy"
Your mouth stays shut tight.
It won't convey feelings
Of joy or delight.

Say, "Hppy. I'm hppy,"
And say it all day.
Will others believe that
You are what you say?

Your smile will look faulty
If A's disappear,
And rhyme becomes flawed
If you grin ear to er.

It wouldn't be right
To be left without A
'cause "straight" would be "stright"
Veering rightly astray.

Just look under "L"
For "Alaska" and "All"...

...and keep looking all day
For Three A if you stall!

Eliminate A's
And then Oakland's a loser.
Their A's could be "Q's"
Or "The Which?" or "The Who's?" or

"The 'postrophe Esses" –
Could that be a team?
No, better the name of a
Grammar class theme!

44

If A weren't for Apple
There'd be no "disaster"
For that would be "disster",
A syllable faster.

Do **you** think that "sister"
Began as "sisaster"
When A's were more common
And language was vaster?

I think that a "saster"
Could be an ex-sister
Whose sister days passed her
And nobody missed her.

This is Landon's painting of a saster. Obviously,
she's gone.

"Awesome" is "wesome"–
I once was just "mesome".
Shesome made twosome
And then we were threesome.

Our firstone was lonesome,
She wanted one moresome;
We had to agree some
So we became foursome.

48

"Austin" would be "ustin".
To you that may not matter.
Read the dedication.
You see, Austin is our daughter!

(Our other daughter, London,
Whose name I didn't say,
Has only been discluded
'cause she didn't get an A.)

Until, aha, her middle name
It's lovely, "London Vale",
And here you see how I contrive
To claim we didn't fail!

The continents use lots of A's
To start and then to finish.
Lacking A's in front and back
Their grandeur does diminish.

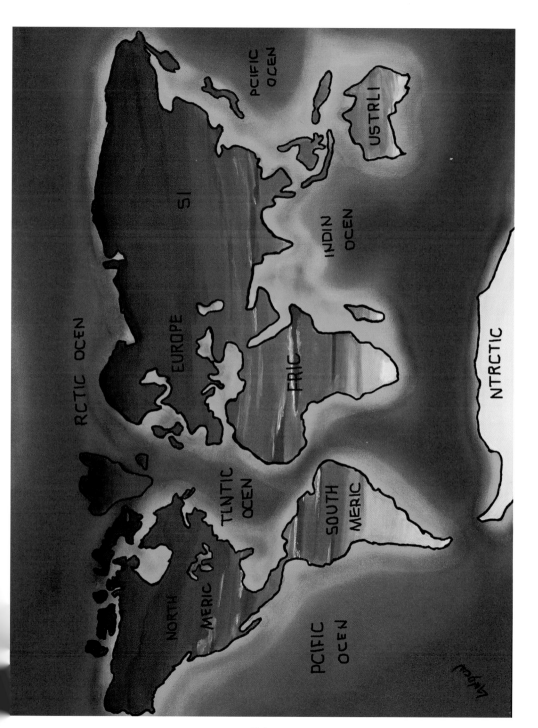

54

"Able" isn't "able"
Because it morphs to "ble".
And though it seems a shame,
You know it can't be –
Its a shme.

"Mon Lis" is Mona Lisa.
(I submit this only wittily.
It couldn't happen in real life.
They love their A's in Italy.)

"meric" for "America"
Just doesn't have the ring.
From sea to shining sea, you see,
It's A's that make her sing.

Three dozen states
Are spelled with A's,
Nineteen have two or more;
In Arkansas, Alaska, three;
In Alabama, four.

Maine would be Mine.
Thats fine if you're ME.
I save me an A
And get a state... free.

Sea

Low Sea

Middle Sea

Shining Sea

Ludpou

60

"Abacus" would be 'b'cus
B'cus I don't know why
You'd choose an abacus these days
To add or multiply.

Fishing wouldn't be a test
If "bait" were always "bit".
You'd have to buy a bigger boat
In which your fishes fit!

If you'd go subtracting A's
You might not go so well...
Like, if you go, like, to L.A.,
You might, like, go to L.

"Airheads" would be "irheds".
Would they really know the difference?
...

...

ir
molecules

If A weren't for apple
Then what would we see
If we went to the orchard
And looked in a tree?

Those red orange and yellow
And green things that grow –
Would they still be apples
Or what? Do we know?

Yes,

A **must** be for Apple.
It's always been that way.
Apples keep you healthy.

72

You should eat one every day!

Well, that's what I said
Up on top of that hill,
And when I was finished
The crowd stood there still.

It seemed that my speech
May have been all for nil,
All my fervor for A,
All my heart, all my will

A-9

Until suddenly someone
From out of the chill
Cried, "I cast my vote for
Christopper T. Hill!"

A-11

And then came another
And more followed those
'til everyone shouted
From up on their toes,

"He's right, A's for Apple,
And he'll fit the bill –
Let's ALL cast our votes for
Christopper T. Hill!"

The End

A-13

Coming Soon...

If Two
Weren't
A Pear

By Christopper T. Hill

To Order: Call 1-800-662-7753

"If Two Weren't a Pear" is a book of poems (pears, like apples, **are** pome fruits, if you want to get scientific about it) by Christopper T. Hill with colorful art panels. It is one of the author's favorites. Here is a sample poem to show you how carried away he got this time.

If Two's Weren't Pears
By Christopper T. Hill

If two's weren't pears
Nor bakers dozens
Would ducks be geese
And sisters cousins?
Would bankers beg
For bricks to loan
To fruit that's played
Instead of grown?
And if we worked
At playing fruit
Would wise be fools
And fools astute?
Would music taste
Just like it sounds
And spoons be notes
And notes be pounds
And if you ate
A quarter-note
You'd suffer only
Quarter-bloat
And if you paid
A pound per quarter
Stems would play
A dollar shorter?
If once upon
Was not a time
And words were wood
And orange wood rhyme
Would rhyming woods
Who toot to fruit
Pay bricks a buck
Or ducks to flute?
Wood spoons you ate
Tune into sounds
And bloat their notes
In quarter-rounds?
Would begging bankers
Play like fools
On fruit-grown music
Yielding jewels?

No, two's <u>are</u> pears
And wood ducks quack
And sisters have
Their sisters back.

or visit www.topperhill.com

Coming Soon...

I L A V 8 2 0 I 0 ...

Jay figured to fly into Cleveland (461 miles,
742 km) non-stop, then hang around for a
puddle-jumper to Toledo Express Airport.
That's how it worked out, too. But I still
don't know how he knew Katie would be in
Toledo.

... 42C   KT

Coming Soon...

Frank was a kid. That alone is not unusual. Most kids are. What made Frank unusual is that he could <u>see</u> things. Now do you see why Frank was special? Either do I. Don't we all? Not really. See, Frank could see things that were <u>really</u> <u>there</u>. Not just things that weren't. Or, let me see. I think he didn't see what he <u>saw</u>, he saw what <u>was</u>. Did you ever notice that <u>was</u> and <u>saw</u> are <u>saw</u> and <u>was</u> backwards? Either did I. But Frank did. See, saw. Saw, was. So, what. Right?

Well, Frank didn't think so. So. He just went right on seeing what <u>was</u> instead of what he <u>saw</u>. One day, and this is only for instance, oh, and before I tell you, let me tell you that Frank was just like any other kid, which is that he was so busy all the time that he couldn't do everything in the world but could only do what he was doing at the time. As we know, time is so scarce for a kid that what a kid is doing at the time takes up so much time that the time he has to do everything else in the world is so scarce it gets fairly obvious that he isn't going to get everything else in the world done. Do you see what I'm saying? How <u>do</u> you? I know. You're a kid, too, and you have the exact same problem, so I'm just telling you exactly what you already know. If so, just erase everything I've already said because you already know it, and I will proceed to tell you the for instance I was telling you about, as long as you agree to believe:

A) That Frank was just like any other kid,
B) That Frank found it difficult to do more than he was doing <u>at</u> <u>the</u> <u>time</u>, and
C) that seeing what <u>was</u> instead of what he <u>saw</u> was something that he had to squeeze in <u>while</u> he was doing what he was doing <u>at</u> <u>the</u> <u>time</u> and <u>while</u> he was being just like any other kid.

Now, I am fully aware that it's hard to agree to believe in three things just plain old automatically. We should all be skeptical and analyze things before we just go off believing things that someone says we should believe. Do you believe that? I do. So, just to make up for the fact that it's asking alot to have you agree to believe three things all at once, I will make it more simple. But first, I'll make it more complicated by working it out with you just how unlikely it is that you would agree to believe all three things at once just automatically.

First, you could refuse to believe any of the three.
Second, you could agree to believe A, but not B or C.
Third, you could agree to believe B, but not A or C.
Fourth, you could agree to believe C, but not A or B.

or visit www.topperhill.com